TEENAGE MUTANT NINJA TURTLES™

THE SANTA SNATCHER

by Jane E. Gerver
illustrated by Patrick Spaziante

Ready-to-Read

Simon Spotlight

New York   London   Toronto   Sydney

Based on the TV series *Teenage Mutant Ninja Turtles*™
as seen on Fox and Cartoon Network™

SIMON SPOTLIGHT
An imprint of Simon & Schuster Children's Publishing Division
1230 Avenue of the Americas, New York, New York 10020

Manufactured in the United States of America

First Edition
2 4 6 8 10 9 7 5 3 1
Library of Congress Cataloging-in-Publication Data
Gerver, Jane E.
The Santa Snatcher / by Jane E. Gerver ; illustrated by Patrick Spaziante.– 1st ed.
p. cm. – (Ready-to-read) (Teenage Mutant Ninja Turtles ; #4)
Summary: When the Turtles hear a Santa snatcher is on the loose, they try to
catch him, before he spoils Christmas for the city.
ISBN 0-689-87018-3 (pbk.)
[1. Heroes–Fiction. 2. Santa Claus–Fiction. 3. Martial arts–Fiction.
4. Turtles–Fiction.] I. Spaziante, Patrick, ill. II. Title.
III. Series. IV. Teenage Mutant Ninja Turtles (Series) ; #4
PZ7.G3264San 2004
[E]–dc22
2004000892

Christmas was coming, and
the Turtles were getting fat.
"These cookies are good!"
said Leonardo.
"Hey, leave some for Santa!"
Splinter scolded.

"How does Santa get to every house in just one night?" asked Donatello.

"And what's up with his reindeer?" wondered Michelangelo.

"How do they fly?"

Splinter shook his head. "My sons, it is better not to ask such things," he said.

"Maybe the reindeer are mutants like us," said Raphael. "Let's find out!"

"Shh," said Splinter, pointing to the TVs.
A TV reporter announced, "Someone
in the city is trying to catch Santa Claus.
He is known as the Santa Snatcher!"

"That will ruin Christmas for everyone!"
Splinter said.

"Come on, guys!" said Raphael.

"We have to catch the Snatcher

before Santa gets snatched!"

The Turtles packed some disguises and climbed into their Subway Buggy. Off they rode through the sewers under the city. **Zoom!**

"Do we have a plan?" asked

Michelangelo.

"We will trick the Snatcher,"

said Leonardo.

"How do we get to the North Pole?"

Raphael asked.

"Do not worry. We will start

closer to home," Donatello told him.

The brothers got out of the buggy.

Donatello and Leonardo went one way.

And Michelangelo and Raphael

went the other.

Donatello set up a big pot and a sign.

Leonardo put on a red suit,

black boots, and a long white beard.

"Ho, ho, ho! Merry Christmas!"

he called out.

Just then a man came walking by,
holding a huge sack.
"Season's greetings, Santa!" he hissed,
before trying to throw the sack
over Leonardo's head.

Suddenly a boy shouted,

"That's not a real Santa!

He's too skinny!"

"Oops!" muttered Leonardo.

"Forgot the pillow!"

The man ran down the street.

He was the Santa Snatcher!

Donatello could not catch him.

Leonardo grabbed his katana swords.

But he could not get them out

of his Santa outfit in time.

The Santa Snatcher got away!

What could the Turtles do now?

Meanwhile Michelangelo and Raphael
went to Green's Department Store.
They took the escalator up to Toy Town
where a long line of children
were waiting to meet Santa.

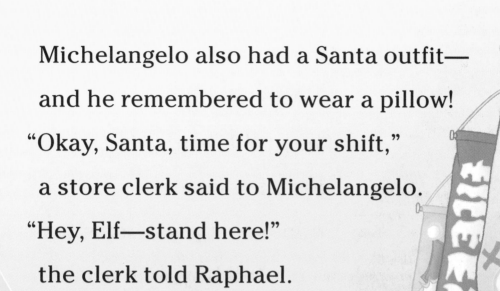

Michelangelo also had a Santa outfit—
and he remembered to wear a pillow!
"Okay, Santa, time for your shift,"
a store clerk said to Michelangelo.
"Hey, Elf—stand here!"
the clerk told Raphael.

One by one, the children sat
on Michelangelo's lap.
They told Santa what
gifts they wanted.
Soon it was a tall boy's turn—
a *very* tall boy with a sack!

He was the Santa Snatcher!

Raphael pushed in front of him.

"Um, Santa's busy," Raphael told him.

"Why don't you tell **me** what you want?"

"Out of my way, Green Elf!"

the Snatcher snarled.

Michelangelo twirled his nunchakus.

"Come here, little—uh, big boy!"

he said. "I will tell you

what you are getting for Christmas!"

But once again the Snatcher

was too quick.

The Snatcher ran out of Toy Town.

"Hey, wait!" Raphael shouted.

He ran to the escalator

and slid down the side.

But the Snatcher was gone . . . again!

Michelangelo and Raphael
saw Leonardo outside the store.
A huge crowd had gathered.

"A parade is coming!"

said Leonardo.

A marching band played

as people waved at a float.

"Ho, ho, hello!" Mrs. Claus called.

"Where's Santa?" someone yelled.

"He's home with the reindeer,"

replied Mrs. Claus.

The float stopped in front of the Turtles. Raphael spotted someone in the crowd— he was the Santa Snatcher!

"The Snatcher is going after Mrs. Claus!" Raphael whispered.

"We have to stop him!" Leonardo said.

"But how?" asked Michelangelo.

The Snatcher wiggled through
the crowd. Then he climbed up
onto the float.

Suddenly Mrs. Claus began to dance.
She twirled her baton.

But it wasn't really a baton—
it was a bo staff!

"Don!" his brothers shouted.

The Snatcher started to throw his sack
over Donatello.

But Donatello was faster.
With his staff he knocked
the Snatcher into a fake fireplace!
"Ow!" the Snatcher cried,
as he bumped his head.

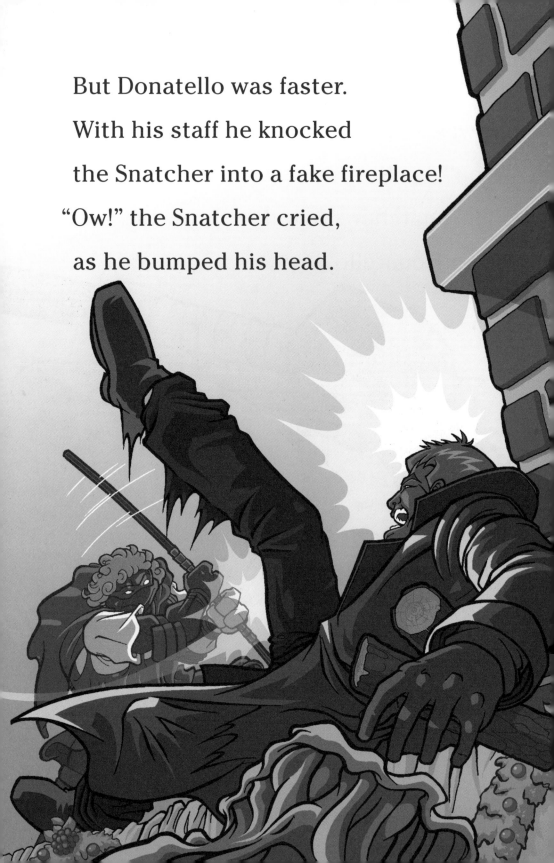

The other Turtles climbed
onto the float.

"Good job, Don!" Leonardo said.

"Had enough holiday fun?"
Raphael asked the Snatcher.

Soon everyone in the city had
heard the good news.
The Santa Snatcher would not
snatch again!
The Turtles headed home.

"We didn't find out how reindeer fly,"
Michelangelo told Splinter.
"Or how Santa goes to every home
in just one night," added Donatello.
"And we forgot to get you a gift!"
said Leonardo and Raphael.

"Do not worry about that,"
Splinter said kindly.
"After all, you made the city safe
for Santa. And that, my sons,
is the best present of all!"